Snowball Trouble

MW01060393

by Kate Howard
illustrated by Stephen Gilpin

Scholastic Inc.

ISBN 978-0-545-75839-0

Text copyright © 2015 by Kate Howard
Illustrations copyright © 2015 by Stephen Gilpin

Published by Scholastic Inc. SCHOLASTIC and associated logos are trademarks and/or registered trademarks of Scholastic Inc.

10 9 8 7 6 5 4 3 2 1   15 16 17 18 19/0

Printed in the U.S.A.   40

First printing, January 2015

It was January. The kids in Room 222 were back at school after two weeks off.

"Welcome back, second grade explorers!" said Mr. Bug. "I hope you all like hot cocoa. You'll need it to keep yourselves warm this week. It's time for our Winter Festival!"

"What is Winter Festival, Mr. Bug?" asked Milla.

"It's my favorite week of the year," said Mr. Bug. "We'll start our science unit on weather. The best way to learn about weather is to get out and explore it!"

"But it's freezing out there!" said Ruby.

"Mr. Bug?" said Henry. "I know a cool trick that we could try as a class."

Henry whispered his idea to Mr. Bug.

Mr. Bug smiled. "Good idea, Henry!"

Everyone put on snow pants and jackets. Then they followed Mr. Bug outside. It *was* freezing!

"Let's start with Henry's idea," said Mr. Bug. "Please stand back. I don't want anyone to get hurt."

Mr. Bug held a cup full of boiling water.
He stepped forward and tossed it into the air.
"Poof!" The water turned into snowflakes!

"Wow!" yelled Abby. "Is that magic?"

"Yes," said Mr. Bug, "the magic of
science!"

Back inside, Mr. Bug explained how the trick worked. "When it's very cold outside, there isn't a lot of water in the air. But boiling water has a lot of vapor, or water that has turned into steam. When vapor hits the cold, dry air, it clings to tiny particles and turns into crystals! That's how the boiling water turned into solid flakes."

"And *poof*!" said Milla. "Instant snow!"

"I just read a book about snow," said Abby. "It starts as water way up in the sky."

"That's right, Abby," said Mr. Bug. "Cold air turns the water into ice crystals. Each crystal has a unique shape. That's why no two snowflakes are alike."

Mr. Bug held up a paper snowflake. "When it's cold and there's a lot of water vapor in the air, that's when it snows."

"Water way up in the atmosphere turns to ice crystals. Then the crystals grow six arms." Mr. Bug wiggled his arms in the air.

"Like a monster?" asked Diego.

"Sure! I guess we could call snowflakes ice monsters," laughed Mr. Bug.

"Over time, more water vapor collects on the ice crystals and freezes. When the crystals get too heavy, they fall from the sky." Mr. Bug dropped his snowflake.

"As the crystals fall to the ground, they stick together and float down as fluffy snowflakes."

"So what does all this have to do with our Winter Festival?" asked Diego.

Mr. Bug grinned. "This week, we'll use frozen ice crystals—"

"You mean snow?" asked Henry.

Mr. Bug nodded. "Yes, we'll use snow to create big, strong structures."

"We're going to use snow from the playground for a classroom challenge," Mr. Bug explained. "You'll be working in teams all week long."

"Each team will work together to build an amazing structure out of snow and ice. The team that makes the best structure will be named our Winter Festival Champions."

Mr. Bug winked. "We'll celebrate our champs at the party on Friday."

"Who picks the winner?" Diego asked.

"I will," said Mr. Bug. "I want to see snow structures that are strong. And there will also be extra points for imagination."

Mr. Bug read the names of the kids on each team. Milla, Abby, and Diego were on one team. Henry and Ruby were on another.

The class split into groups and began drawing plans for their snow creations.

"I think we should build a snow maze!" said Diego. "Then we could make a map and hide treasure in the maze."

"Great idea," said Abby. "Let's do it!"

Across the room, Henry and Ruby were planning their own ice structure.

"Mr. Bug loves bugs," Henry said. "What if we make an ice caterpillar?"

Ruby nodded. "Or a turtle. We could make a turtle shell out of ice and snow!"

After lunch the next day, the second graders headed outside.

"Let the Winter Festival fun begin!" Mr. Bu said.

Each group got a big pile of snow to build with. They also got shovels and pails.

Diego asked if they could use water, too. "Water will help melt our snow to turn it into ice again. And ice is stronger than snow!"

Mr. Bug nodded. "Good thinking, Diego. You can try it. Let's see what happens when you combine snow and water."

Diego dumped a bucket of water on a pile of snow. Then he stomped on it to mix it all together.

"Oh no," Milla moaned. "Our snow pile is a slushy mess!"

Abby slipped on an icy patch. "Whoa!"

Henry and Ruby still hadn't decided what to build.

"At least we don't have a big mess," Henry said. "Diego's looks like a slushy moat."

"Hey, that gives me an idea!" said Ruby. "What if we build a snow castle?"

"Cool!" said Henry.

Milla, Abby, and Diego worked together to mix their slush with new snow. Then they began to build the wall of their maze.

Ruby and Henry's icy castle was coming along nicely, too.

The next day, the groups had more time to work on their projects. All the sculptures were starting to look great!

"Hey, this is perfect snowball snow," Diego said.

"Don't get any ideas, Diego," Ruby warned.

After school, Mr. Bug's students ran out to the playground.

Diego and Milla looked at Henry and Ruby's creation. "This wall would make a perfect fortress for a snowball fight," said Diego.

"You're right!" Milla cried. She tossed a snowball at Diego. "Gotcha!"

Diego laughed and fired one back at her. Soon other kids got in on the action.

A big snowball came flying at Diego. "Snowball fight!" he yelled.

Splat!

Snowballs went flying in all directions.

Using Henry and Ruby's castle wall for cover, Diego made dozens of snowballs.

"Hey, Milla!" he called. "Heads up!"

Milla laughed. She and Ruby formed a team. Henry and Abby made another team. Everyone threw snowballs as fast as they could.

A snowball flew at Diego. He dove for cover behind Henry and Ruby's wall.

Crash!

"Oh no!" Ruby yelled.

"You broke our castle wall!" howled Henry.

"I'm sorry," Diego said. "It was an accident."

"It's totally ruined," sighed Henry.

"We'll never win now," Ruby said.

"Mr. Bug is going to be upset," Milla said.

"Now we won't get to be champs," Henry moaned.

Ruby looked like she was going to cry.

Suddenly, Diego smiled. "I'll help you fix this, I promise. I have an idea."

"If we all work together, we can build something even better," said Diego.

"Better than our castle?" Henry asked. "I don't think so. Our castle was the best."

"It was great," Diego agreed. "But if we work together, we can build an even *bigger* castle."

When the kids told Mr. Bug about the snowball fight, he wasn't happy. But he did like Diego's plan.

The next day, the kids got back to work. Milla and Ruby dug a moat. Abby and Henry made more snow bricks. And Diego carved a little dragon out of snow!

Soon, the new castle was almost done.

Abby stepped back to admire it. "We just need a way to get across the moat."

"A bridge!" yelled Milla. "Let's build a snow bridge that will hold us all!"

The kids finished the bridge just in time.
"It's time to pick a winner," Mr. Bug said.

"Let me take a look at this snow castle and see how my second grade explorers did."

Mr. Bug walked around the outside of the castle. Then he peeked over the edges of the walls.

"You can go inside the castle, Mr. Bug," said Henry.

Milla nodded. "The bridge will hold you!"

"How can I be sure?" asked Mr. Bug.

Henry waved Diego, Abby, Milla, and Ruby over. They all stood on the bridge.

"See?" said Diego. "This is the best snow fortress ever!"

"Indeed it is," agreed Mr. Bug. "I think we have a winner!"

"Congratulations!" Mr. Bug said. "You're all winners because you worked together."

"If we're all champions, then who's going to celebrate us at the party?" asked Diego.

Henry grinned. "Guess it's you, Mr. Bug!"

Mr. Bug laughed. So did all the kids in Room 222.